WHEN SKIES HAVE FALLEN

A SNOWY BALL

DECEMBER, 1981

Debbie McGowan

Beaten Track
www.beatentrackpublishing.com

A Snowy Ball
Published 2017 by Beaten Track Publishing

Copyright © 2017, 2018 Debbie McGowan

ISBN: 978 1 78645 197 2

Cover Design by Debbie McGowan
Images used in cover:
Bosmanerwin: Dancing Children
https://pixabay.com/en/dancing-children-love-cute-light-2972960
Jill111: Snowflake Background
https://pixabay.com/en/snowflake-snow-snowing-winter-cold-554635/
(Pixabay – Creative Commons Licence)

Beaten Track Publishing,
Burscough. Lancashire.
www.beatentrackpublishing.com

Contents

Thursday, 10th December 1

Friday, 11th December.. 7

Saturday, 12th December: 0800 hours 17

Saturday, 12th December: 1000 hours 25

Saturday, 12th December: 1400 hours 31

Saturday, 12th December: 1600 hours 39

Recipes 49

About Debbie McGowan.. 57

By Debbie McGowan.. 58

Beaten Track Publishing.. 60

Thursday, 10ᵗʰ December

"Looking ahead to the weekend, the cold spell continues, with severe frost throughout London and the southeast, and up to twelve inches of snow expected in the next twenty-four hours.

"All in all, we're in for a fairly settled few days due to high pressure over most of the British Isles, with occasional depressions over the English Channel bringing further flurries of snow. Will we see a White Christmas? That's a strong possibility. This is London's snowiest December in over a hundred years..."

"Dickens has a lot to answer for," Arty muttered. He poked the darning needle through the sock's heel and tugged it through the other side, and again, before he snapped off the yarn with his teeth. The meteorologist's joyous forecast had irked him as if the man himself were responsible for the imminent blizzard. Alas, the view through the sitting room window only served as confirmation; it had been snowing for several hours—large, dry flakes that had stuck and blanketed everything in minutes—and it showed no signs of stopping. Perish the thought it might continue for the next forty-eight hours, let alone the next two weeks.

Still, White Christmases were rarer than hens' teeth; in Arty's sixty-two years, he had witnessed three at most, only one of which he'd considered remotely joyous. It was in the late twenties, and he'd have been eight or nine years old—young enough to be thoroughly invested in the winter wonderlands of Dickens' imagination. To an able-bodied child, there was nothing quite so magical as waking to snow on Christmas morning, when there were no chores to be done nor school to attend; the day was theirs to spend as they would—snowball fights, building snowmen, sledding…

"It was a death trap." Arty shook his head and chuckled to himself, recalling the terribly rickety contraption Uncle Bill had constructed that year from a couple of lengths of woodworm-riddled skirting board held together by a prayer. He'd attached a rope to it, with the dog on the other end, and shouted 'mush!', naively expecting their rather clever though profoundly stubborn collie to move. Instead, Shep had wandered around to the side of the sled and cocked his leg over it.

Undaunted, Bill had untethered the dog, and the four of them—Bill, Arty, his sister Sissy, who had been given Christmas Day off work, and the dog—had set off in search of a decent slope to descend. It had been no easy feat, either, in the largely flat local terrain, and in the end, they'd joined at least two dozen others in repeatedly sliding down the railway embankment until dark clouds and a fresh downpour sent them home, rosy-cheeked and numb-fingered, for their Christmas dinner.

By Boxing Day, they'd been completely snowed in—it had been relentless—and Bill had brought out the playing cards, systematically winning all of Arty's festive treats, only giving them back when Sissy threatened to blacken his eye—all in jest, Arty liked to think. That was also the year Bill had fallen through the thin ice covering the fishing pond in a somewhat fortunate failed attempt to persuade Arty and Sissy they could safely use it as a shortcut to the church.

He'd been a sod for it, had Bill, goading Arty into all kinds of dangerous pursuits which had terrified him—more so in hindsight—though he'd never been brave enough to say so. That his mother had entrusted her young brother with the care of her offspring—when Sissy was barely a year younger than

Bill and far more responsible—had made little sense to Arty at the time, though he understood now.

At the sound of the front door opening, Arty abandoned both his daydreaming and darning and swiftly rose, switching off the TV on his way out of the room. He stopped in the doorway to watch Jim, bent double just inside the front door and fighting to get out of his boots. "Hello."

Jim glanced up and offered Arty a weary smile. "Hey."

"You're early."

"Yeah. We had to stop work. Too damn cold." Jim straightened and began unbuttoning his coat, or tried. He was making very slow progress. "What's the weatherman have to say?"

"More to come, I'm afraid. Here, let me." Arty moved in and took over, hoping only he was conscious of his racing heart. The way Jim was watching him at close quarters, it was impossible to say, and Jim had asked more than once if there was something Arty wasn't telling him. Thank goodness he only had to keep the secret for one more day. He'd never done well at hiding things from Jim. "No wonder you're struggling. Your hands are freezing."

"Care to warm 'em for me?" Grinning mischievously, Jim sneaked one hand under Arty's pullover. Arty gasped in shock, instinctively trapping Jim's hand with his elbow and keeping it there while he unfastened the rest of the buttons.

"There," he said sternly, taking a step back and rubbing at the palm-sized cold spot Jim had left on his side. "Do you want to eat first or go for your bath?"

"Bath, I think. Warm up a little. Hey!" Jim called; Arty was already moving towards the bathroom. "I can deal with it myself. You go rest."

Arty laughed. "That's what I've been doing all day, love." That wasn't strictly true; he'd baked, prepared dinner, finished the ironing and most of the sewing, but it was all very sedentary and for no reason beyond those being the more pressing of the household tasks. In spite of Arty being registered disabled, of the two of them, he was in better physical shape, and it was telling on the eve of Jim's retirement.

Jim should have retired two months ago, when he'd turned sixty-five, but who was going to enforce it when he was his own boss? He'd only relented now because his knees had had it; Charlie's back was in much the same state but he had a few years to go yet. Their doctor was trying to bump Jim up the waiting list—Arty could only hope he didn't succeed in the next fortnight.

For all of that, and ignoring Jim's pained expression, Arty took his word for it that he could run his own bath. "I'll turn the oven down and make some tea."

"Great." As they passed each other, Jim reached for Arty again, but he dodged out of the way, laughing at Jim's disappointed scowl. Excellent as the heating was in Dalton Place, he found it difficult enough to stay warm without Jim's icy hands to contend with.

In the kitchen, he filled the kettle, checked on the casserole and turned the oven down as low as it would go before returning to the sitting room to tidy away his darning kit. The next time Jim put his heels through this particular pair of socks, they'd be heading for the dustbin, however difficult pure wool socks were to come by. There were only so many times Arty could darn his prior darning, even if it did mean having to forgo teasing Jim for being a skinflint and refusing to part with his demob socks. Not that these were his demob socks; those were long gone, and Arty was still getting around to breaking the news to Jim, though he suspected Jim was already aware, for nor had he asked.

He returned to the kitchen and made the tea, in his head going through the schedule for the next two days. There were things he needed to do and he couldn't do any of them until

Jim had left for work in the morning or else it would ruin the surprise—a surprise which had been a year in the making. Arty put the cosy on the teapot and listened for the sound of water sloshing to gauge whether Jim had closed the bathroom door. He couldn't be sure and decided not to risk contacting Joshua to warn him of the impending blizzard. The telex machine made a hell of a racket and going through the operator took far too long. Besides, the snow would fall regardless of whether Joshua knew in advance.

It turned out to be a wise decision as Jim emerged from the bathroom less than five minutes later, his enduring mop of hair, these days as white as the heavy flakes drifting past the window, shown off to startling effect against his lobster-red complexion. Briefly, he entered their bedroom; drawers opened and closed; Jim whistled some ditty or other and arrived soon after in pyjamas, dressing gown and slippers.

Arty fetched the clean ashtray, accepting Jim's nod of thanks, and poured the tea. "To think, after tomorrow, you can do this as much as you like."

"Yeah," Jim agreed though his frown indicated he had more to say. He packed the bowl of his pipe, lit it and inhaled, momentarily disappearing behind the chuffs of aromatic smoke, speaking once they'd cleared. "I said I'd go in next week if the snow causes problems."

"You can't." The words were out before Arty could stop them. "I mean…" He cleared his throat, delaying.

"You already got my days planned out, huh?" Jim joked.

"Well…there's the bedroom wallpaper that I'd hoped to get up before Christmas." Arty had bought the paper a few weeks ago because it had been on sale for half price, but he had no intention of redecorating this side of the New Year and could manage it perfectly well on his own, though it would be a more pleasant task if they did it together.

Jim watched out of the window—snow-covered roofs as far as the eye could see—and crooned the first two lines of Irving Berlin's 'White Christmas', segue-ing into, "All these years and I've seen only one English white Christmas."

Arty chuckled. "Funny you should mention it. I was trying to think earlier when the last one was."

"Wasn't it the year Joshua and Susan got married?"

"Was it?" Arty searched his memories of Joshua's wedding. "Yes, I remember now. It was piled high either side of the church path, so it would've been the year before." The wedding had been in January 1971, but the December snow had taken a while to melt.

"Almost eleven years ago…" Jim mused. He relit his pipe and returned to gazing out of the window, his thoughts elsewhere. Joshua's wedding was when Jim and Joshua had last seen their mother and when Arty had met her for the first time. Seventy-five years old and completely undaunted, she'd travelled alone, all the way from West Virginia, and she was as wonderful as Arty had imagined—hardy, funny and full of beans—Jim was very much like her. Of course, both sons had tried to convince her to stay in England, but she wouldn't have it.

"We should go visit," Jim said. "Once my knees are fixed."

"Yes, we should," Arty agreed steadily—no easy feat when his heart seemed to want out through his ribcage. Jim turned from the window with a smile, which Arty somehow reciprocated.

"Awesome." Jim set his pipe in the ashtray and rubbed his hands together in anticipation. "All right, what's cooking, good-looking?"

Holding back his sigh of relief, Arty seized both the oven gloves and the opportunity to escape Jim's attention. Tomorrow couldn't come soon enough.

Friday, 11th December

"Arty? Are you there?" Icy air blasted through the letterbox along with Jean's call. Quite why she was shouting through it, Arty didn't know; Jean and Charlie lived in the apartment upstairs.

"It's open," he said on his way down the hall. He turned the knob and pulled; the door didn't budge.

"I think it's stuck," Jean said.

"Apparently so." Yet Jim had left for work barely half an hour before, and the door had opened no trouble at all. "Give it a push," he instructed.

"I am!" It put up a fight, and when it finally gave, it sprang wide open, sending Arty staggering backwards. Jean stumbled sideways into the hall, bringing half a snowstorm with her.

"Don't wait for an invite, Jean," Arty joked. Jean's eyebrows rose. "Where have you been this early in the day?"

"I stayed at Eddie's. I didn't much fancy driving home in the snow."

"Come on through to the kitchen—the stove's been on all night." Too cold to wait, he dashed off before she'd removed her coat. He filled the kettle, calling back, "I wish we'd done the cash-and-carry trip on Monday, like we planned." The weather had been brutal all week—rain, gale-force winds— and they'd put off the trip as long as they could, but tomorrow was their dance school's Christmas party, and it would happen, snow or no snow.

"Yes, well, we weren't to know, were we?" Jean arrived, minus her coat, simultaneously unwinding her scarf and massaging her shoulder. The pain showed on her face.

"What have you done?" Arty asked.

She gave him a look. "Charged a door?"

"Ah." Arty chuckled and shooed the cats from the top of the stove so he could put the kettle on. It earned him a mean glare from Suky, who immediately leapt to the table and made a bed out of Jean's newly removed, therefore still warm scarf. Meanwhile, Sam jumped straight back onto the stove and Arty caught a whiff of singed cat hair. He hoisted the animal to safety, keeping hold of him and one-handedly preparing the teapot.

Of the dozen or more cats they'd shared their home with over the years, Sam was, beyond doubt, the one with the least common sense. If he wasn't on the stove, he was trying to climb on top of the gas fire or getting himself locked in the airing cupboard. At least twice Arty had almost tumbled him with the laundry, which made it all the more surprising that at seventeen, Sam was the most long-lived of their cats. Jim insisted kindly the old chap felt the cold, hence he was also a house cat; more likely, Arty thought, he didn't know how to operate the cat flap.

When the kettle began to whistle, Arty put Sam on the floor and quickly turned off the flame, but for once the cat seemed to have understood and went off in search of somewhere else warm—and hopefully safer—to sleep.

"Mince pie with your tea, Jean?"

"At this time of day?" She made a point of examining the clock; it was a little after eight in the morning.

"Baked yesterday afternoon," Arty tempted.

"Oh…why not?"

"That's the spirit."

"One can only imagine," Jean murmured knowingly. Arty's mincemeat was infamous for both its decadence and its potency. The recipe, which had come from a fondly remembered elderly neighbour who had passed away some years ago, was a glorious concoction of dried fruits and diced baking apples, steeped overnight in two tablespoons of rum, sherry or brandy, or so the recipe said. Arty chose to interpret the 'or' as an 'and'—the more the merrier was his Christmas motto and a reason to celebrate of which he would never tire.

The pies were all more or less the same shape and size; even so, Jean picked carefully from the box Arty held in front of her, her eyes widening as she sniffed the spirit-laced air. "I'd best have just the one," she said.

"The pastry might be a bit on the short side."

"Jolly good." She bit into it, cupping her hand to catch the crumbs, and groaned.

"Up to par?" Arty needn't have asked; her reaction said it all, and he was both relieved and delighted. Every year, he baked this first batch of pies for the Christmas dance, and every year he worried they wouldn't meet his usual standard. He'd have asked Jim to test them, but they'd have been half gone already.

"Mmm. I'd say so." Jean placed the pie on the plate Arty had left for her and swallowed what was in her mouth. "Has Joshua been in touch?"

"Not yet. I expect he has everything under control."

"Other than the weather." Jean's remark prompted them both to look out of the window. The ridge of snow on top of the garden wall was easily six inches deep.

"I'll give him a call when we get back," Arty said. "How are the roads?"

"Not awful. The gritting lorries were out in force first thing, and the main road is mostly grey slush."

"That'll freeze by this evening."

"Yes, it will," Jean agreed. "We should get going as soon as we can."

Arty nodded and poured the tea so they'd be ready to leave at nine when the shops opened.

***

The cash-and-carry was chaotic to say the least. It seemed half of London had come to stock up in preparation for the harsh spell meteorologists were predicting, though it had been less a forecast than a statement of fact, seeing as it was already snowing. Jean had to park quite a distance from the entrance to the large, draughty hangar-turned-warehouse, and the walk back was treacherous, but thankfully without incident.

Arty collected a flat-bed trolley from the bay and followed Jean up and down the aisles, pausing when commanded to do so and taking the opportunity to rub his gloved hands together. His breath misted in front of him and his toes stung; he was certain he'd have been no less chilled had he remained outside, but he wouldn't miss this for all the world.

"Party rings are always popular," Jean said, loading six boxes, each containing three packets, onto the top of the already impressively full trolley.

"Yes, they are." Arty smiled, picturing the children tomorrow, adorning their fingers with the iced ring biscuits. There was an awful lot of wastage, but it was worth it for the fun they had. "Have you made the trifle?"

"No. I thought I'd buy one this year." Jean set off again.

"Buy one?" Arty was horrified. "You can't buy one."

"It's such a faff."

"But your trifles are…not to be trifled with."

Jean glanced dolefully over her shoulder. "I've got the grandchildren overnight. Perhaps you could make one."

"A grandchild or a trifle?" Arty asked wryly. Jean slowed down so she could nudge him with her elbow. He made a show of grimacing in pain, and they both laughed. "You could always leave them with Uncle Arty and Uncle Jim for the night," he suggested.

"The lengths you'll go to for a trifle…"

"Not *just* for a trifle. You'll be busy preparing this lot." Arty nodded at the trolleyful of food. He also not so secretly loved having the children over.

"As will you."

"But Jim won't."

"Ah, I see. You're volunteering Jim for babysitting duties. I hope he realises it's the shape of things to come."

Arty didn't deny it. "I need to distract him, Jean. You know how he is."

"Hmm, yes, I do. A very astute man, is your husband. I wish I could say the same about mine."

"Charlie doesn't do so badly," Arty defended lightly.

"You would say that," Jean muttered but didn't elaborate. It would be something or nothing; it always was. Charlie could be a thoughtless so-and-so at times, but after forty years, Arty felt compelled to speak up on his friend's behalf if only because Jean expected it. "If you meant it," she said, "about having Lucy, John and Ella…"

"In return for a trifle…"

Jean laughed. "Then they're all yours." She slowed at the end of the aisle and looked over their purchases. "That's everything, isn't it?"

"Where's your list?"

Jean tapped a finger to her temple.

"In that case, yes. That's everything." Arty manoeuvred the heavy trolley towards the row of cashiers and joined the shortest queue, which still put them eighth in line.

"All those empty shelves," Jean remarked.

Arty looked behind him; the sight was astonishing, with entire aisles, normally stacked from floor to well above eye level, now expanses of bare grey. His gaze wandered up to the roof and along the arched lattice trusses to the remains of a vast pulley that would once have been part of the aircraft lifting gear. He'd had terrible trouble with the one in his hangar back at RAF Minton, resulting more often than not in having to work with the craft on the ground. The speed at which he could shimmy under a fuselage was, apparently, legendary.

These days, he could do with a pulley to get himself up off the floor, never mind a Vickers Wellington. Such wonderful memories—of the group captain's weekly walk-by calling 'as you were' that constituted a formal inspection, of Charlie's daily requirement for Arty's spanners... The clangs of tools echoed in his ears, and he was there once more, jollying along his trainees. *Right, lads, let's get her up and see what we can see...*

"Arty?"

"Hm?" He turned back to find Jean had unloaded the entire contents of their trolley onto the conveyor belt. "Sorry. I was miles away."

"I noticed. Minton, perchance?"

"Yes." He chuckled, a little embarrassed at being caught out, with the added advantage that the rush of blood to his cheeks had left him warmer than before. "You know me far too well."

Jean affectionately squeezed his arm, forgiving his momentary nostalgia, and then wheeled the trolley into position on the other side of the cashier, ready to reload. This time, Arty helped. When they were done, Jean paid the bill from the dance school subs, and they braced in anticipation of facing the weather.

"Oh, goodness!" Jean stuttered to a stop outside the entrance. "Can you remember where we parked?"

Skidding, Arty gripped the trolley handle and just about stayed on his feet as he drew up alongside. He blinked the snowflakes from his lashes and squinted at the uniform mounds of white, under which, somewhere, was Jean's car. "I believe it's that one." He pointed to a larger mound at the end of a row. "Or…that one."

Jean sighed and hooked her arm through his. "Come on."

He had little choice but to go with her. "Are you sure you can drive in this, Jean?" The pressure tightened on his arm until he winced.

"I'm going to forget you asked me that."

"Good," Arty said.

***

They made it back to Dalton Place in one piece, but that was as far as they were getting. It had taken two hours to make the twenty-minute journey and they'd witnessed several fellow motorists come a cropper. It was hairy at times, but in spite of his earlier lapse in judgement, Arty had felt safe with Jean behind the wheel. She was an exceptionally skilled driver. Nevertheless, she let out a tremendous sigh of relief as she stopped the car and pulled on the handbrake. At the same time, the front door to the house opened; Jim and Charlie emerged and came out to the car to help unload.

"You go in and make the tea," Jean advised.

"If you're sure…"

"We'll need it. Besides, don't you have a call to make?" Jean tilted her head meaningfully towards the men at the back of the car.

"Good thinking." Arty got out and trudged as swiftly as was possible past Jim and Charlie towards the house. He was interested to know why they were home from work so early, but it could wait. Shutting the door behind him, he crossed the sitting room to the telex machine and typed a short, somewhat cryptic message: *Jim home. AOK?* Then he waited, anxiously chewing his lip, for a reply. He was so intently focused on the machine that he almost jumped out of his skin when the phone rang. "Hello?"

"Hello, Mr. Clarke, it's Daniel."

"Ah, good afternoon, Daniel." He was Joshua's interpreter, though not normally outside of his work with the Royal National Institute for the Deaf, where he was developing a telex-type phone specifically for deaf people.

"Mr. Johnson asks me to inform you that flights to and from Heathrow airport have been cancelled for the rest of the day."

"Damn it." Arty heard the front door open and kept his voice low as he asked, "Does he have a contingency plan?"

"He most certainly does. Mrs. Johnson Senior is presently en route to Manchester Ringway, due to land at 2300 hours. A car has already been despatched."

"Good old Joshua…" Arty murmured.

"Arty? You in there?" Jim knocked on the sitting room door.

"Pass on my thanks, Daniel. Bye." Arty quickly replaced the receiver and donned his most innocent smile as he opened the door. "Yes, I am. Why? Did you miss me?"

"Darlin', you know I always do. What—"

"How come you're home?" Arty nipped Jim's query right off at the bud. "Too cold again?"

"That, and we got no work. We figured the cabbies know where to find us if need be."

"You're still going to the pub to celebrate, though, aren't you?"

"Once it's open." Jim narrowed his eyes. "You trying to get rid of me?"

"Not at all." Arty affected a laugh—a double bluff, he hoped, because Jim's question hadn't been a serious one. "I'd hate for you to miss out on a celebratory pint on account of inclement weather."

"Don't you worry about that." Jim took Arty's hand and led him towards the kitchen. "You gonna come with us?"

"I'll come for one. I've offered to have Lucy, John and Ella overnight. There's no need for you to rush back. We've got everything for the party, and I can't make the sandwiches until tomorrow. I do hope Santa will make it."

"He's all set—so he tells me," Jim said with a wink.

Arty glanced back at the red suit hanging in the hall and smiled to himself. Another decoy successfully executed.

Saturday, 12ᵗʰ December
0800 hours

"With a record eleven inches of snow on the tarmac, the airport remains closed until further notice..."

At the sound of the bedroom door opening, Arty switched off the kitchen radio and opened the book he'd been reading since the early hours. Between excitement and his usual battle with restless legs, he'd hardly slept and was glad, in a way, that Eddie had been snowed in, thus they hadn't had the pleasure of Jean's grandchildren's company overnight.

Ever a creature of habit, Jim used the bathroom, returned to the bedroom for his slippers and dressing gown, went back to the bathroom to put in his eye drops and finally arrived in the kitchen looking as if he'd been sobbing for hours.

"Morning, love," Arty greeted, shifting his bookmark from its prior location—around fifty pages back and he recalled nothing of what he'd read—before he set his book aside.

"Good morning, darlin'. Bad night?"

"I've had worse," Arty dismissed and rose from his chair.

"You stay there. I'll make the breakfast."

"Oh, you will, will you?" Arty drummed his fingers on the table in feigned contemplation. "What do I fancy?" Predictably, Jim had already taken out the frying pan and eggs. He passed behind Arty on his way to the cupboard where they stored their dry goods. Flour in hand, he passed a second time, and

17

Arty caught hold of his dressing gown belt. Jim stopped and allowed himself to be reeled in.

"Pancakes OK?"

Arty tugged Jim close enough to grip a handful of his lapels, peering up into Jim's face as it came down to his. They kissed, slowly and gently though enticing enough for an early Saturday morning. Arty was in half a mind to suggest they forget all about breakfast and go back to bed. Alas, those small triangular sandwiches wouldn't make themselves.

With a reluctant, frustrated sigh, Arty released Jim. "You have quite a kiss on you…for an OAP."

Jim chuckled. "You'll catch up soon enough, Arty Clarke, don't you kid yourself." He moved away to make the pancake batter. "I didn't check if we had syrup."

"Yes, we have," Arty confirmed. He was out of his chair before Jim could draw the breath that would inevitably have fuelled a request he stay put. Jim let the breath go and set about whisking the batter, singing and intermittently whistling 'A Marshmallow World'. Arty retrieved the maple syrup Joshua had brought back from his last business trip some two years since and put it and two sets of cutlery on the table.

While he was up, he prepared the coffee percolator—a Saturday morning treat—and fed the cats, impressed by how calmly he was going about their usual routine. By now, Jim and Joshua's mother would, with all good wishes, have arrived in London, safe and sound, and Arty was resisting the urge to chance a call to confirm that were so. He'd waited this long; it would be a very poor do if his impatience ruined everything at the last minute.

He was also second-guessing the decision to keep it from Jim. It had been Joshua's idea, and Arty suspected an element of mischief was involved, although it had not dawned on him before. Jim and Joshua were very close—best friends as well as brothers; the times Joshua had used his political influence to come to Jim's aid were too numerous to count—not least when he'd tried to get Jim released from prison back in '54. Indeed, he'd succeeded, but on condition Jim be extradited. Joshua had visited the prison to tell him, and Jim had flatly refused.

Arty had been privy to none of this until much later, and only then via an overheard conversation. Had he known, he'd have told Jim to accept the ambassador's offer. A life alone was a small price to pay for Jim's freedom. But Arty had been given no say. Jim had served his time, and Joshua had been there for the both of them, then and ever since. Arty didn't doubt the sincerity of Joshua's benevolence, not at all. Even so, it hadn't gone unnoticed that it always put Joshua in a position of power over his brother. Fortunately, he wasn't the kind of man to abuse that position.

"Where's your head at?" Jim's murmur, right next to Arty's ear, lured him out of his thoughts.

"Oh, you know…" He nodded towards the window. "This snow…the dance. I hope the children can all get there." It wasn't entirely a lie; the dance was on his mind too.

"Well, if push comes to shove, I'll ask Joshua if he can send his driver."

"Imagine that." Arty smiled, amused. "A Bentley cruising the council estate."

"What's that kid's name? The tall one with all the freckles."

"Tommy O'Shea?"

"Yeah, I think so. His classmates give him hell for dancing."

"Yes, that's Tommy."

"Maybe I'll send the chauffeur for him anyway." Jim flipped the pancakes onto a plate and handed it to Arty. "All right. We're good to go."

"Where's your—ah." He hadn't noticed the other plate complete with its own stack of pancakes. "I really must stop daydreaming."

"Then you wouldn't be you," Jim humoured. "Come and eat before it gets cold."

Typically, the moment they sat down, the phone rang. In spite of Jim's defunct knees, he was still quicker off the starting block than Arty, who set down his fork and clasped his shaking hands in his lap as he listened to Jim's side of the call.

"We're eating breakfast … Sure! … All right. See you, bye." Jim ended the call and returned to the kitchen, deep frown lines extending the full width of his forehead.

"Is everything OK, love?"

Jim resumed his seat, still frowning. "Not sure. That was Daniel—Joshua's guy? He said they'll be here in an hour. Joshua needs to talk to me about something. Daniel didn't say what." Jim sliced a chunk from one of the pancakes and ate it dry.

"Aren't you going to put syrup on those?" Arty asked.

"Huh? Oh, yeah." Jim took the bottle and tipped it absently.

"Jim…"

He stopped. "Oops." His pancakes were absolutely swimming.

Arty sighed. "Oh dear. This is backfiring horribly."

"What?"

"I know…why Joshua is coming over. He's got you a retirement gift."

"That all?"

Arty smiled glibly. "It's a lovely gift. I'm sure you'll be very pleased with it."

"Well, why didn't he say so instead of leaving me to think all kinds of crazy things?" Jim's worry had turned to anger, which he took out on his breakfast, jabbing furiously into the pancakes and leaving ragged edges that darkened as they absorbed some of the copious syrup. But he was never cross for very long, and by the time Arty poured the coffee, Jim was almost back to normal—he even managed to laugh at the pool of maple syrup that remained on his plate.

"Man, I hope Joshua's got business in the States sometime soon. Hell, I might just tell him he's gonna have to go, seeing as this is all his fault."

Arty laughed but could think of nothing to say. After thirty-seven years, awkward silences were rare between them, and he was glad that only he seemed aware of it. Jim remained distracted as he prepared his pipe and lit it, and merely glanced in Arty's direction when they heard the letterbox bang shut and the newspaper hit the floor. He was usually out of his chair faster than a greyhound from a trap and then hobbled back, tight-lipped and brave-faced.

"I'll get it," Arty said, rising and leaving the room. "You should probably shower before you get caught up reading."

"Why?" Jim asked when Arty returned.

"We're expecting visitors."

"It's Joshua."

"Yes, but what if Susan and the children are with him?"

Jim looked down at his dressing gown. "I'm decent."

"Jim!"

"All right, all right. I'll go get a shower. Can I just…" He made a grab for the newspaper, but Arty whisked it out of his reach. Jim laughed. "You're really cracking the whip this morning."

"Ha. I haven't even started." Arty folded the newspaper in half and tucked it under his arm. "I'm popping up to see how Jean's getting on. Shan't be long." When he reached the door to the stairs, he added, "Go and shower."

"I'm on it."

Arty took Jim at his word and continued up to Jean and Charlie's apartment. They called it that, though, in truth, the ground and first-floor apartments were interchangeable. When the three of them had originally moved into Dalton Place towards the end of 1945, Arty had still been struggling to walk, thus he had taken the ground-floor apartment, where Jim had joined him the following year, and Jean and Charlie had taken the first floor. After their son Eddie was born, they'd swapped apartments, and then, when Jim's knees started giving him trouble, they'd swapped back.

The top floor they rented to a couple in their thirties—a gay couple and proud to call themselves such. Arty had been subjected to the word as an insult too many times to embrace it the way the younger generation seemed to have done, as had Jim to a certain extent, out of necessity, given his continued involvement in campaigning for rights. For a while, he'd talked about retiring from politics, too, but the reports in the American press earlier in the year, of homosexual men dying from rare diseases, had renewed public interest in the private lives of those they'd 'permitted' to exist without fear of persecution for their 'sickness'. Now there was a very real danger of ending up back where they'd started, and Jim and others of their generation refused to stand by and let it happen.

As for their top-floor neighbours: they saw very little of them. Both worked long hours in the city; they paid their rent on time and kept to themselves. Ideal tenants.

Jean and Charlie's front door opened as Arty reached it, and Charlie exited with head down, almost walking straight into Arty.

"Bloody hell. You frightened the life out of me."

"Sorry, Charlie. Good morning."

"Yeah. Same to you," he muttered and dodged past to scurry away down the stairs. Arty knew exactly what that would be about; he could smell the pastry baking, and Jean would've had poor Charlie on vol-au-vent filling duty the moment he got out of bed.

"Is that you, Arty?" Jean called and appeared in her hallway, connected oven gloves on her hands. Arty shut the door and joined her in the kitchen, eyeing the multiple baking trays and mountains of vol-au-vent cases, some empty, some filled.

"Hard at it already, I see."

"Yes. Almost done, actually. And I made your blasted trifle even though you welched."

"I did not!" Arty protested. He couldn't very well look after the children if they weren't there to be looked after.

"No matter. Eddie's going to walk them over for the party this afternoon, so you can make up for it then." Jean grinned smugly. "Anyway, are you staying long enough for a cuppa?"

"I'd love to, but…" Arty paused to release a pent-up breath. "Joshua's coming at ten o'clock."

"She made it?"

"I assume so—that's why I'm here. May I use your phone?"

"Help yourself."

"Thank you." Arty retraced his steps to the phone in the hallway and picked up the receiver, temporarily bamboozled. Jean had installed one of those trim phones with buttons rather than a dial, and Arty abandoned his first attempt, quite sure he'd misdialled or, more accurately, mistyped the number. His second attempt, he listened to the ring tone with baited breath.

"Joshua Johnson's residence. Daniel Frodsham speaking."

"Hello, Daniel, it's Arty Clarke."

"Ah, yes. Good morning, Mr. Clarke. Mr. Johnson anticipated your call. His mother has arrived and all is well."

"Goodo."

"Did you wish to speak with her?"

"No, no. That's fine, Daniel. Thank you. I'll see them all at ten."

"You will, Mr. Clarke. Bye for now."

"Bye." Arty returned the receiver to its cradle and turned to smile at Jean, who had been listening from the kitchen doorway. "She's here," he confirmed, laughing in relief.

"That's wonderful," Jean said, smiling broadly. "Now…have you made those sandwiches?"

Arty left without another word.

Saturday, 12th December
1000 hours

At a little before ten o'clock, the Johnson clan en masse descended on Dalton Place. Joshua, Susan and their four children—two adopted, two fostered—remained near the car so as not to upstage Mrs. Florence Johnson, eighty-five years of age, tremendously jet-lagged…and as spritely as ever. Arty walked out to greet her, having left Jim in the kitchen making tuna and sweetcorn sandwiches and as yet unaware that their visitors had arrived.

"Y'all couldn't have waited till I got here before you dumped all this snow?"

Arty laughed. "You don't like it, Florry? I'll send it back immediately and demand a refund." He offered his arm to her, which she accepted, and they set off carefully up the hastily cleared path to the front door. As they reached it, Arty moved forward and held it open for her.

"Why, thank you." She bowed demurely, making light, though Arty could see she was a little nonplussed by the fuss.

"We don't get many visits from VIPs, Florry."

"Tsh," she dismissed. "Ain't nothing important about a decrepit old fool like me. Now where's that son of mine?" Straightening her back, she took a big breath and hollered, "Jimmy?"

There was a kerfuffle in the kitchen, and what sounded very much like a chair falling over, before Jim lurched into view.

"Momma? What the…?" For a few seconds, he gawped, jaw hanging, and then a mile-wide smile broke out, along with tears as mother and son moved together and embraced in a sobbing mess right in the middle of the hallway.

Arty wasted no further time in beckoning Joshua and his family in out of the cold, greeting each with a signed 'hello' as they edged past Jim and his mother to reach the sitting room. Daniel brought up the rear; the chauffeur had remained in the car.

"Is he driving back?" Arty asked.

"No. He's going to collect Mrs. Tomkins' grandchildren so they can attend your party."

"How thoughtful."

Daniel nodded in acquiescence rather than agreement. He and Geoffrey—the chauffeur—were on Joshua's staff and did as they were told. Arty hadn't yet fathomed why Daniel had been drafted in for the weekend, although he realised soon after when Joshua's youngest emerged from the sitting room and asked if she could use the bathroom.

"Yes, come," Arty said and signed and led her down the hallway, pointing to the appropriate door. She thanked him, and he returned to Jim and Florry, who had pulled themselves together a little in his brief absence.

"You understand the signing?" Florry asked.

"Some," Arty confirmed.

"See, Momma? Told ya."

"See what, Jimmy?" She winked at Arty, who smiled bashfully. On her last visit, Jim's mother had gushed over Arty, telling anyone who'd listen how wonderful he was, and hugging and kissing him repeatedly. It hadn't been a shock, particularly; he'd been subjected to Jim's and Joshua's open affections for almost four decades. However, since Joshua and Susan's wedding, Arty and Florry had written often, and she'd promised not to 'suffocate him with love' this time around, but…life was short, and he was being terribly British. Without further ado, he approached her with arms open, and with a delighted smile, she went into them.

"Guess I was wrong and I'm very important after all."

"The *most very* important," Arty said sincerely. "It's so lovely to have you here, Florry." He didn't dare say more, aware of Jim's gulps behind him and not sure if he was going to laugh or cry himself.

"Yoo-hoo! May we come in?"

"Jean." Reluctantly, Arty released his mother-in-law and reinstated his stiff upper lip. "Yes, do," he called.

Jean and Charlie stepped into the hall, the latter carrying a bottle of cream sherry, which he presented with a flourish to Jim's mother.

"Oh my! You remembered."

"Too right, I did. And I got a couple in, just in case."

"A couple?" Jean scoffed.

"Half a dozen," Charlie confessed.

"Oh, jeez. Now we're in trouble," Jim said with a playful wink at Arty that perfectly matched the one Florry had given him earlier, and he had a point. At the wedding reception, Florry had been on the schooners, and by the end of the evening, she was merry-going-on-legless. British cream sherry had become her favourite tipple, and Charlie had promised to stock up for her next visit, adding cheekily that he wouldn't say no to a bottle of finest West Virginian bourbon, should she wish to return the favour.

"That's mighty kind of you, Charlie. I think I got a little something in my suitcase for you."

Charlie rubbed his hands together. "That's tonight sorted, then."

"Hey, Mom, don't suppose you got any maple syrup in there, do you?"

"Maybe I do. You're just gonna have to wait and see. Now, what's a mother gotta do to get a cup of coffee around here?" She eyed each of them in turn, finishing on Arty.

"I'll do that now, Florry." Before he got that far, Joshua came out of the sitting room at the same time as his daughter came out of the bathroom, and she watched in bewilderment as Joshua signed something at his mother.

"I came to see the both of you," Florry replied curtly. Joshua signed something else, by which point his daughter was standing beside him, staring at his hands and shaking her head. The next thing, the pair of them were gabbling at speed.

"What's that about?" Charlie asked.

"The gist…" Arty watched them for a moment and then shrugged. "They're talking too fast."

"Mom and Joshua have their own kind of sign language," Jim said. "Georgette wants Joshua to teach it to her."

"You can follow that?" Arty asked, as impressed as he was astounded.

"You can't?" Jim teased with a grin. "Come on. I'll help you make that coffee and then we'll all sit down together—" he made sure to turn so Joshua could read his lips "—stop my little brother's nose getting put out of joint."

Everyone laughed at Joshua's dramatic indignation. He had this way about him that was a curious mix of the reserve more typical of the British—perhaps from his many years spent working with government—and wide gesticulations, even when signing, which Arty assumed were equivalent to Jim's booming voice and larger-than-life mannerisms.

What Arty hadn't seen before, however, was Joshua displaying envy towards his brother and vying for their mother's attention because, of course, on her last visit to England, it had been all about Joshua. Still, she seemed to have it in hand, and one didn't need to understand the Johnsons' unique dialect of sign language to know she was giving him a dressing down.

When she was done, Georgette nudged her sulking father to get him moving, and at last they all made it out of the hallway and into the sitting room, with the exception of Arty and Jim, who went to the kitchen. Arty took the kettle over to the sink to fill it, smiling as Jim stepped up behind and slid his arms around Arty's waist.

"You're a sneaky one, Arty Clarke. How long have you been planning this?"

"Since last Christmas." Arty turned off the tap and shuffled sideways, with Jim behind him, to the stove. "Where's Sam got to?"

"I locked him in the bedroom. He stole half a can of tuna. I only looked away for a second or two."

"And you say I'm sneaky," Arty complained. He turned to face Jim and held his gaze. "You're not cross, are you? About it being a surprise."

Jim smiled. "Not at all. Thank you." He kissed Arty on the lips with a little more fervour than was wise with almost their entire family in the room next door, and it got Arty all a-fluster. Jim eased off, whispering, "I love you, darlin'."

"And I love you," Arty whispered in response, the months of tension leaving him in an instant. He could gladly have joined the cat in the bedroom for a nap. Alas, there would be no time for napping today.

"Right, men." Jean marched into the kitchen and stopped in front of them. "We've got four hours to get ourselves and all the food to the hall. I think we need to organise the troops, don't you?"

"Aye, Sarge," Arty and Jim answered in unison and grinned at each other.

"That's agreed, then," Jean said, fighting a smile as she marched back the way she'd come, calling, "As you were."

Saturday, 12th December
1400 hours

"Would you look at the state of us? We're like a couple of old men." Arty veered towards the wall on the corner of the street and rested the plastic box on it. Jim stopped alongside, groaning as he flexed his knees.

"I hate to tell you, darlin', but we *are* a couple old men."

"Speak for yourself," Arty grumbled, though his heart wasn't in it. After all his bravado that they could manage the half-mile walk to the hall, they'd made it as far as the corner of their street—twenty-five yards at most. Loaded with food and dredging their feet through part-frozen, deep snow was hard going, and Arty had been a fool to turn down the lift from Jean. It would have meant making two trips, which was inconvenient, but that wasn't why he'd refused, and seeing Jim suffer had really driven the point home.

"I'm sorry, love. This is my fault."

"What's your fault?"

"Us, clapped out in the snow. I'm ashamed to admit it, but Joshua's attempts to monopolise your mother's attention got the better of me." Indeed, he was so ashamed it took quite an effort to raise his head and meet Jim's gaze, anticipating he'd be angry, or at best perplexed. He was neither. "I'm glad you think it's funny."

"This is all about Joshua? You guys have been best buddies for years."

"Yes, and I realise now I'm acting just as childishly as he is."

"Didn't you and Sissy ever compete for your mom's affections?"

"Not really. She was a difficult woman to get close to. Dad…yes, a little, perhaps, but he never treated us the same, because of the age difference, and with Sissy being a girl. His expectations for her were low and she surpassed them all, whereas I failed him in every regard."

"Oh, Arty…" Jim's expression was sympathy and apology rolled into one.

"Don't feel sorry for me. I intentionally pitted you against your brother."

"You're making it sound far worse than it is."

"I wanted to show your mother that you were still the strongest and fittest of her two sons."

"You did, huh?" Jim adjusted his stance, frowning and smoothing a gloved hand over his chin. After several moments, he sucked his teeth resolutely, and said, "All right. Here's what we're gonna do. We're gonna flag down the next cab that passes and give your kids the best damn party they ever had. Then, after Santa's visit, you and I are gonna take to the dance floor and show that little brother of mine just what we're made of. What d'ya say? Are you with me?"

A shiver ran straight down Arty's spine, and it had nothing whatsoever to do with the cold. Yes." He smiled. "I'm with you…until death do us part."

"If a cab doesn't hurry along, that might be sooner than you think."

***

The hall Jean and Arty leased for their dance school was on the first floor above a nightclub, and while small, it was perfectly suited to their needs, which was why, even though they could have afforded somewhere larger, they'd chosen to remain in the same space since the very beginning, in January, 1950.

Like all businesses, the dance school had seen its share of ups and downs; the seventies had proved particularly tough, sustained only by the old die-hards. More recently, there had been a surge in the number of younger people taking up lessons. Latin and ballroom was enjoying something of a renaissance, it seemed, especially among those looking for love. Some found it in the dance hall, just as they always had. Others danced on in lonely pursuit of that one special person they intended to woo. If ever they lost heart, Arty told them his and Jim's story, or Jean and Charlie's, and how, in the face of tremendous adversity, the magic of the dance had seen them through.

As their cab stopped outside the building, Arty peered up at the windows and the warm glow of coloured lights blurred by banked snow. "The power's still on, thank goodness." He'd had a moment of panic on the way and convinced himself Jean and everyone would be standing outside a building in darkness.

"We best get inside," Jim advised. "The kids are coming."

"Already?" The party didn't start for another half an hour, but sure enough, several children were eagerly pulling their parents towards the door. Jim paid the cabbie, and with boxes in hands, he and Arty followed the early birds inside and upstairs to the hall.

"Good heavens, it's chilly in here." Arty blew air from his mouth, mortified to see it vaporise. He set his box down on the nearest chair, quickly exchanged boots for shoes, and went to check the radiators.

"The heating's on, believe it or not," Jean called from the other end of the room, where she had everyone hard at it. Charlie and Joshua carried a table over and hovered, awaiting instruction. "Put it next to this one, please," Jean said as she turned to direct Susan, armed with a stack of the small tins of Quality Street each child would receive at the end of the party, over to the stage. Meanwhile, Florry fought with a box of party ring biscuits.

"She's gonna love those," Jim confided to Arty and then in a louder voice asked, "You need some help, Momma?"

"No, thank you," she replied as the plastic inner sleeve popped open and several biscuits tumbled onto the plate below. She picked up a pink one, examined it—"This looks yummy"—and took a bite, crunching with slow deliberation before she gave her verdict. "Tastes yummy, too." She eyed the stack of boxes and nodded in satisfaction.

Arty chuckled. "Like mother, like son, eh?" They rarely had shop-bought biscuits at home, because whenever they did, Jim would consume the entire packet in one sitting, and party rings were among his many favourites.

"I'm gonna go check they're safe to eat." Jim handed the box of mince pies to Arty and moved off.

"I'm sure they're perfectly fine."

"You can never be too careful." Jim grinned and continued on his way, resting one hand on his mother's shoulder, with the other snatching a biscuit before she had a chance to stop him.

"Jimmy! Those are for the little ones."

"Uh-huh?" He put the entire thing in his mouth, smiling around it, and brushed his mother's cheek as if to remove crumbs. She slapped his hand away—all in fun.

Watching them, Arty felt so warm inside he forgot how cold it was in the room until a child's voice asked, "Mr. Clarke, please can we keep our coats on?"

He peered down at Rosie and her friends and smiled. "Of course you can, sweetheart."

The little girls trouped past, making a beeline for the chairs along the side of the hall, just like the WAAFs back at Minton. It was a truth Arty had realised over the years—the times changed, the fashions came and went, but some things were reassuringly constant. Soon, the boys would arrive, and they'd loiter near the food tables, bottles of pop in hands, watching the girls and waiting for a signal—a small smile sent their way, a moment's restlessness, a whisper or a giggle…

Would you care for this dance?

These days, the girls were just as likely to make the first move, and a good thing it was, too. Some of those poor women at Minton waited months for a clearly interested yet shy suitor to garner the courage and ask for a dance. Arty remembered it all too well; were it not for Charlie asking Jean on his behalf, and then Jean encouraging him to take a chance, he might never have got to spend the best years of his life with Jim by his side.

"Are you going to bring those sandwiches over or do I need to come and get them?"

At Jean's sharply spoken words, Arty stacked one box on top of the other and carried them over to the tables where everything was beautifully laid out on silver platters—everything other than the sandwiches and mince pies. Arty popped the lid off one of the boxes and began arranging the small triangles on the remaining empty platters, aware of Jean watching him closely. He glanced sideways at her. "What?" he asked.

Her expression softened. "Are your legs bad today?"

He chuckled guiltily and blushed. "No. They're fine. I just seem to…have a lot on my mind."

"You were daydreaming, you mean?"

"Er…yes," Arty admitted.

Jean sighed in minor exasperation and turned to lean against the table, looking out along the hall. "Eddie's arrived. That will give you something to do." As she said it, the fast light thud of tiny dance-shoe-clad feet advanced on their location, and two little arms clamped around Arty's left leg.

"Uncle Arty!"

"Hello, Ella." Arty pivoted carefully and smiled down at Jean's youngest granddaughter. "What a beautiful dress!"

"It's got sparkles. Look." She released Arty's leg and spun on the spot, the glitter in her skirt creating a wheel of multicoloured specks that spun with her.

"You'll make yourself dizzy, Ella," her father warned, but she paid no heed, and when she did finally stop, she staggered away like a miniature drunk. Arty was laughing and watching with one eye shut as she miscalculated and bumped into one of the older children.

"Ella…watch it!" Lucy—Eddie's eldest—scolded and huffed to her friends. At fourteen, Lucy was a bit of a handful for her parents though whenever she was at Dalton Place, she behaved impeccably. All of a sudden, she noticed Arty watching her and made eye contact. He smiled and raised his hand to acknowledge her and got a flicker of a smile in response.

"Right, what time are we up to…" He checked his watch—ten minutes to three—and did a quick head count. "Looks like almost everyone's here, Jean. I'll put some music on."

With Jean's nod of agreement, Arty went over to the booth where they kept the record player and records. He selected one of the Christmas albums and set it up to play the third track: 'Walking in a Winter Wonderland'. It was a good tune to warm up with—a fast foxtrot, slow jive or just a general free-for-all. As long as it got them moving, Arty wasn't fussed, although a few of the teens moaned and groaned while they were about it, having just walked through a winter wonderland for real, and the little ones were far too excited to do anything other than run around in circles chasing each other.

Arty didn't want to spoil their fun, but he could see an accident happening soon unless they settled down. Fortunately, Jean was on hand to encourage them to cha-cha to the next song—'Here Comes Santa Claus'—as opposed to skidding on their knees, although Arty had seen Jim pull that move a good many times in his hay day.

Needless to say, knee slides were no longer part of Jim's repertoire, not that he needed to do anything particularly impressive to charm the socks off his dance partner and anyone else who happened to be watching. Presently, he was dancing with Ella, who adored her Great-Uncle Jim, and given half the chance would monopolise him all afternoon.

Alas, time was getting on, and when Jim next turned his way, Arty tapped his watch. Jim gave him a thumbs up. At the end of the current dance, he bowed graciously to Ella. Predictably, she clung to him, begging him to dance with her again and even pouting when it was clear she wasn't going to get her own way.

"I sure hope Santa's not watching," Jim warned lightly.

Ella gasped. "Santa's coming!" Her declaration triggered a rush of excited whispers all around the dance floor.

"All right, already," Jim said loudly. "Lemme go see if he's here yet."

Saturday, 12ᵗʰ December
1600 hours

"You got 'Santa Claus is Coming to Town' over there, Arty?"

"I have, Florry. Shall I put it on next?"

She raised her half-full glass to the light, held it there just long enough to admire the rich, deep-red hue of the sherry and then knocked it back in one go. Arty covered his mouth to stifle his surprised laughter.

"Lemme get a refill," she said, and off she went. A minute later, she was back with a full glass.

"I take it he's ready?" Arty asked.

"Who?"

"Santa. Who else?"

"Santa?"

"Isn't that why you asked me to play the song?"

She cackled and slapped Arty's arm. "Heck, no. I was gonna ask you to Charleston with me."

"Charleston?" Arty stuttered over the word as if he'd never heard of it before.

"Don't tell me you don't know how to Charleston."

"It's been a long time." At least fifty years, in fact. It was the Roaring Twenties when his aunt had taught him to dance, so naturally, he'd learnt the Charleston, but he hadn't done it since. "I might be a bit rusty," he said, never mind that it was one of the most physically challenging dances. After his earlier

39

failure at mere walking, he might need a few sherries himself before he chanced it. "Are you sure Jim won't mind?"

"Mind? Why would he mind?"

Arty didn't think he would, but he was stalling, trying to come up with a way of letting Florry down gently without admitting aloud he wasn't up to it. He glanced around the room for a sign of Santa Claus, but Jim had only just left, so he was out of luck. He did, however, catch Joshua's mocking shuffle-step and smirk in his direction, accompanied by the exaggerated mouthing of *dumb hoofer*. Now that really was a step too far…and all the motivation Arty needed.

"Florry, I would be honoured to Charleston with you."

"Honoured, you say?"

"Yes, honoured." And more than a little nervous, so much so that the previous song had ended and he had yet to choose another, but it mattered not, for the silence was immediately filled with a deep, cheery, "Ho, ho, ho…Merry Christmas, children," as a familiar red-suited figure strolled into the hall with a large, heavy-looking sack over his shoulder. The youngsters went tearing over and gazed up in awe. Arty sighed; if only Santa had arrived half a minute earlier.

"I must tell you now, children, Rudolph was very glad for those colourful lights. We almost got lost in the snow. I warn him every year…Rudolph, make sure that nose of yours is clean tonight. I need you to guide my sleigh, but will he listen?"

"Poor Santa," one of the children said; Arty had a good idea it was Ella. She was just like her father had been at that age and could hold her own with anyone, even the eminent Santa Claus.

"Oh, ho, ho. Well, I got my elves to make that naughty reindeer a nose-polishing kit, so by Christmas Eve we'll be just dandy. Now…who all's been good this year?"

The more confident children shouted, "Me!" but after so many years, Santa knew the drill. Quite a few of the dance pupils came from poor backgrounds; some lived in dreadfully unhappy circumstances, and Arty and Jean made sure every child received a small gift that might bring them some joy over the festive period. Even the teenagers got something, but not from Santa; their gifts were waiting under the tree in the corner and would be distributed once the younger pupils had taken their turn.

Florry patted Arty's arm to get his attention, and he leaned down so she could speak into his ear.

"Has Jimmy ever told you how I met his father?"

Arty shook his head and kept his gaze on Santa and the children. Jim didn't talk about his father at all.

"Well, like you and Jimmy, it was at a dance."

Arty's heart skipped a beat. He didn't want to listen, and could easily have tuned out Florry's voice, but wasn't this what he'd always wanted? To know more about Jim's father?

"It was 1915, and the socialists had won big—there was a parade to celebrate, followed by a party at the hall. Me and my brother Benjamin had tagged along, and we knew nobody so we were keeping to ourselves. Then this guy comes over, says he's Jimmy Johnson, a member of the party, and he wants to see our cards. Well, Benjamin empties out his pockets, like he's looking for 'em, and Jimmy's tired of waiting but he ain't going nowhere till he's seen our cards, 'cept we ain't got no darn cards. So I did the only thing I could think of…I asked him to dance."

"What did he say?"

"He said yes, of course."

"Now you're going to tell me he was a brilliant dancer," Arty predicted—wrongly.

"No, but he was handsome—tall, blonde…and charming." Florry's eyebrows rose. "Too charming, if you get my drift. A month later, my daddy ordered Jimmy to marry me."

Arty stared at her in horror, but she shook her head, dismissing it.

"I know you'll find this hard to believe after what Jimmy—*Jim* has told you, but it wasn't all on his pop. He was a good man once. We lost that baby in the second trimester, and he loved me in his own way. See, the party always came first with him. After Jim was born, his pop was sent to fight in the war, and he came back a changed man. They called him a traitor for his politics, and he couldn't get a job—he tried so hard to find his way again…"

The rest Arty knew. Jim's father had felt like a failure. He was unemployed, homeless, and while he'd produced two healthy sons, he hadn't seen them that way. Knowing the persecution he must surely have faced as a socialist, it made even less sense to Arty that Jimmy Johnson Senior had punished his wife and sons for their 'shortcomings', and he would never forgive the man for what he'd done to Jim.

"Guess I better lay off that sherry awhile," Florry said, her tone a touch remorseful. Her anecdote had taken a maudlin turn, but it meant a lot to Arty that she'd shared it, albeit with alcohol loosening her tongue.

"Yes, you better had," he said. "If you fall down drunk in the middle of our dance…" He frowned, no idea what he'd do if she did.

Florry chortled. "Takes more than a couple glasses to knock Florry Johnson off her feet."

Across the room, Santa was almost done, with only a handful of children awaiting their gifts. The rest had scattered, leaving a trail of devastation in their wake. Joshua circulated with a black sack, collecting all the ripped wrapping paper. He looked over to the booth and gave Arty another smug grin, to which Arty mouthed, "The tallest elf I've ever seen."

"Dumb hoofer."

Arty's mouth fell open. "Me?" He pointed at his chest.

Joshua nodded and pointed at Arty, then Jim.

"I'll show you," Arty muttered. Joshua cracked up in silent laughter, deliberately goading him, but Arty didn't care anymore. It was a game, a bit of fun, and anyway, he'd soon show him.

Very soon, as it turned out, because Santa was up on his black-booted feet and successfully turned the accompanying grunt of pain into a hearty 'ho-ho-ho'. Arty still winced on Santa's behalf.

"You big kids'll find a little something under yonder tree," Santa announced, and the teens were over like a shot. "Merry Christmas, everybody. See you next year!" And with that, he limped away, waving over his shoulder at the littluns who shouted back, "Merry Christmas, Santa!"

"You got that record cued, Arty?" Florry prompted.

"One moment." He beckoned Jean, who frowned in puzzlement but came to him just the same.

"Yes?"

"Can you take over the record player, please? I promised my mother-in-law the next dance."

"Oh! Of course." Arty and Jean swapped places, and she did a double-take when she saw what was on the turntable. "I was expecting 'Silver Bells' or something of that ilk."

"If only," Arty mumbled as he followed Florry onto the dance floor. "And Jean? Just in case…my will's in the safe."

"Duly noted," she called after him.

"You want me to go easy on you?" Florry asked.

Arty shrugged and moved into position at her side. "I'll leave it up to you." He was optimistic his body would automatically remember what to do when she gave him the steps. In fifty years, it had never failed him, or not in that regard. "It might be wise to avoid lifts, though," he hedged. Florry's reply was a grin that didn't reassure him in the slightest, but the intro had started, so there wasn't much he could do about it.

For the first verse, she kept it simple: a basic left-right and a cross-step and turn, followed by a slide-step and a stop.

"Again," Florry said. Arty readily complied, invigorated by the flapper smiling at his side. "Left, and right, and left, and right, and stop." Florry hoisted her skirt above her knees. "Ready?"

Arty nodded. He'd have to be because that had only been the warm-up, and now the real dancing began. He watched her every move, familiar yet not—a different dance, a different time, but it was all there, in his heart and soul. It was for this he existed, the few minutes of sheer exhilaration when the adrenaline saw off his aches and pains and he was lost to the rhythm and sway of the dance. Each swing back and forth whooshed cool air over his skin. His arms and legs tingled, and it was more than the blood pumping. It was the elixir of life racing through his veins, his youth temporarily restored.

On the next turn-around, Arty caught sight of Jim, standing next to Joshua, both brothers transfixed, though not yet impressed.

"How about that lift?" Arty suggested breathlessly.

Florry grinned. "Don't mind if I do." She wasn't breathless at all, and boy, could she fly! Arty wasn't especially strong, but with a dance partner who knew what they were doing, anything was possible, and their flash moves earned them raucous applause. A few of the pupils joined them on the dance floor, mimicking their steps—even Lucy had put aside her sullenness to dance with Tommy O'Shea.

By the end of the song, Arty was flagging. If he pushed himself too hard, his muscles became so fatigued his legs no longer worked, but he put a brave face on it and made it to the breakdown, trying very hard not to do the same himself.

"Hoo-wee! That was a lot of fun!"

"Florry, you are extraordinary. Thank you for dancing with me."

"No, thank you, Arty. We must do it again sometime."

"Yes," he answered through gritted teeth, consciously driving one foot in front of the other with the singular goal of reaching the chairs along the wall. He'd been so looking forward to dancing with Jim, but one dance was his lot.

He finally made it to a chair; now all he had to do was work out how to bend in the middle so he could sit on the blesséd thing.

"Here, darlin', let me help."

"But your knees, Jim…"

"My knees are just fine." Jim stood slightly astride, bracing so Arty could hold on as he made a controlled collapse onto the chair.

"Thanks, love."

"Welcome." Jim sat next to him, and they watched the dancers together. "So you can do the Charleston, huh?"

"Yes, I can. Only twice in a lifetime, it would seem."

"You get to stay in bed all day tomorrow."

"We're having lunch with Joshua and your mother."

"All right, you get to stay in bed all morning."

"On my own?"

Jim's nonchalant shrug was entirely cancelled out by his wicked grin. "I'm sure the cats'll gladly snuggle down with you."

"Hmm." Arty chuckled but then became serious. "I'm sorry, Jim."

"For what?"

"For getting carried away, and now I'm fit for nought, but I'm sure Jean would be happy to dance with you."

"Hey, I'm perfectly fine sitting it out."

"But Joshua—"

"Is Joshua. Remember what you said when I introduced you to each other? About him looking up to me?"

"Yes. And he still does."

"And I to him. All the incredible things he's achieved—code-breaker, diplomatic aide, teacher, inventor—"

"I get the picture, Jim. Your brother deserves a knighthood."

"And d'you know how he did all that?"

"Because he's clever?" Arty was being facetious, yet Jim's patience never wavered.

"Yeah, he's real clever, but it was Mom's love and determination that gave him a fighting chance to do something with that brain of his. That's why they're so close, and I don't begrudge them."

Arty searched the room until he found Florry and Joshua, standing together next to the party rings, both signing away with biscuits on their fingers. Arty started to laugh. "Jim, look at them." Jim homed in on his mother and brother, shaking his head in disbelief.

"Jeez. Can't take 'em anywhere." He leaned back again and draped his arm around Arty's shoulders. "Are you feeling any better?"

"About Joshua, yes. I think I understand now."

"And your legs?"

"I'll keep you posted."

Another dance came to an end, and Jean raised her voice above the hum of conversation. "Before you take your partners for the last dance of this year's Christmas party, I'd like to make a toast." Jean paused for Charlie and Eddie, who arrived carrying a tray each, one holding glasses of what appeared to be lemonade, the other of champagne flutes.

"Ah, man…" Jim covered his face with his hand and peered between his fingers at Arty. "Did you know about this?"

"I'm afraid so, but I promise it's the last of the surprises… for the time being."

Once Jean had a glass in her hand, she continued with her announcement. "You all know Mr. Jim Johnson—Mr. Clarke's common-law husband and everyone's favourite jive partner.

Today is his first official day as a retiree. Jim, on behalf of everyone at the dance school, I wish you a long and happy retirement." Jean raised her glass and everyone drank a toast and applauded loudly. Jim rose to his feet and took a bow, waving away the few calls for a speech. Before he sat down again, Jean added, "And if you ever fancy helping out..." The applause erupted once more, along with a few whistles. Jim laughed.

"I'll give it some thought."

Jean was all smiles; she knew as well as Arty did that now Jim didn't have the workshop to contend with, wild horses wouldn't keep him away from inspiring younger generations to dance.

Jean rounded off her announcement with, "Mr. Clarke and I would like to wish you all a very merry Christmas and a prosperous New Year. Dance classes resume on Monday the eleventh of January. We look forward to seeing you all then." She lowered the stylus onto the record and left the booth to join Charlie on the dance floor.

"Silver Bells..." Arty leaned against Jim and sighed. "We should be dancing to this."

"There's always next year."

"I suppose." Arty's sadness soon diminished when the dancers stepped off, their festive sparkles scattering across the floor like moon glitter on the ocean. Big or small, beginner or expert, in the eternal ebb and flow of the dance they rose and fell as one.

"You do love a slow waltz, don't you?" Jim teased.

"Regional champions, 1944..."

"Yeah? I think someone may have already told me."

Arty took Jim's hand and gave it a firm squeeze. "What else do old men have but their memories of the good old days?"

"The future?" As Jim said it, Lucy and Tommy waltzed slowly by, though it was like no waltz Arty had ever seen. They continued their snail-pace clockwise circuit, leaving Arty and Jim with a clear view of the entire dance floor where even the little ones were giving it their best, as were Joshua and Florry. As they passed, Florry gave Arty a fake toothy grin and then flinched. Arty looked down and laughed.

"Now I know why I've never seen your brother dance."

"Yeah, he's just a clumsy mathematician with two left feet. But he's got a mean quadratic equation."

"Oh, is that so? See, you're not such a dumb hoofer after all."

"I do OK…for an OAP." Jim twizzled Arty's wedding band between his forefinger and thumb, a comforting, familiar friction that worked in tandem with the gentle waltz, lulling Arty into a daze. It was snowing again; soft, white flakes drifted past the window, starkly beautiful against a sky of deepest blue—a perfectly magical backdrop for their Christmas dance, although now Arty was still, he was aware of how cold it was and how cold he would've been if Jim wasn't there to keep him warm.

"So, Arty Clarke, what are we gonna do with the rest of our lives?"

That was when it fully dawned on him: from here on in, their time was all their own. The realisation made him a little giddy. "Anything you like, love," he said daringly, then in case it was necessary, qualified, "As long as it's not the Charleston."

THE END

Recipes

Here are five recipes for the constituent parts of mince pies and how to put them all together. Mince pies are a traditional British festive dessert consisting of mincemeat (dried fruit, spices and spirits) in a pastry case. They contain no meat whatsoever, although historically, mincemeat did have meat in it.

Mince pies are usually eaten warm with brandy butter, brandy sauce or cream (whipped/double/heavy, doesn't really matter).

Mincemeat

This simple and delicious recipe was given to me by an amazing woman whose coal fire I had the dubious privilege of setting every morning. The recipe was her mother's (she copied it out for me from her mother's original handwritten version) and it's been around since at least 1900.

The mincemeat should be made in October to be ready for Christmas.

Ingredients:
- ½lb (225g) raisins
- ½lb (225g) currants
- ½lb (225g) sultanas
- ½lb (225g) soft brown sugar
- 1lb (450g) grated baking apples (peeled and cored)

- 4oz (113g) candied peel
- 4oz (113g) chopped almonds
- 4oz (113g) chopped suet/vegetable shortening
- 2tbsp (30g) orange marmalade
- ½tsp (2.5g) salt
- 1tsp (5g) ground mixed spice*
- 2tbsp (30ml) rum, sherry or brandy
- Rind and juice of 1 lemon
- ½ grated nutmeg

*Mixed spice is a blend of allspice, cinnamon, ginger, nutmeg, cloves and mace.

Equipment:
- Mixing bowl
- Tea towel/dish cloth
- Sterilised jam jars with lids and covers (you can sterilise with boiling water or a sterilising solution)

Method:
1. Mix all ingredients in a large bowl, cover with a cloth and leave overnight.
2. Stir and put into sterilised jars. Cover with jam pot covers.

Shortcrust Pastry

Proportions tip: this recipe makes enough pastry for 24 mince pies – bases and lids. If you need more or less pastry, keep the proportions of half fat to flour.

Rubbing-in tip: keep hands cool when rubbing fat into flour – shake bowl to bring larger lumps to the surface.

Ingredients:
- 1lb (450g) plain (all-purpose) flour, sifted
- pinch salt (optional)
- 4oz (113g) solid white vegetable fat/lard
- 4oz (113g) butter/block margarine
- iced/ice-cold water

Equipment:
- Mixing bowl
- Sieve (nylon rather than steel)
- Butter knife
- Jug – or something you can pour from
- Tea towel/dish towel

Method:
1. Sieve together flour and salt into a mixing bowl.
2. Add the vegetable fat and margarine/butter.
3. Use a butter knife to cut the fat and margarine into small pieces.
4. Using fingertips, rub the fat and flour together until the mixture resembles fine breadcrumbs.
5. Make a well in the centre of the mixture and add water a tablespoon (15ml) at a time, mixing with the butter knife until the mixture starts to come together into a dough.

6. Press the dough together with fingers – stop adding water once it sticks together in one ball.
7. Leave dough in bowl, cover with a damp tea towel (dish towel) and leave to rest in the refrigerator for 30 minutes.
8. When ready to use, lightly dust work surface with flour.
9. Knead gently and use as required.

Sweet Rich Shortcrust Pastry

The quantities below will create enough pastry for 24 small pies or one large pie. However, due to the need to manually shape the pastry, it is best to use this only for small pies.

Ingredients:
- 1lb (450g) plain (all-purpose) flour
- pinch salt
- 4¾oz (135g) white / golden sugar
- 11oz (315g) cold butter

Equipment:
- Mixing bowl
- Sieve (nylon rather than steel, ideally)
- Butter knife
- Jug – or something you can pour from

Method:
1. Dice butter into small pieces and mix with flour in a bowl to a breadcrumb consistency using fingertips.
2. Add sugar and salt and mix together.
3. Knead briefly into a ball – it can be used straight away or left to chill until later.
4. Work with hands as much as possible as this pastry is very crumbly.

Mince Pies

For the sweeter tooth and a more traditional homemade mince pie, as well as if you have hot hands or are making these with assistance from children, the sweet rich shortcrust pastry is best, as it maintains a crisp, crumbly texture even with hot hands and lots of handling.

Ingredients for 24 small mince pies:
- 1 batch of sweet rich shortcrust pastry or shortcrust pastry (see recipe or buy readymade from shop)
- ¾-1 jar mincemeat (see recipe or buy readymade from shop).
- Milk or beaten egg for glaze

Equipment:
- At least one 12-patty tin
- Rolling pin
- 2½ + 3½ inch pastry cutters – or something you can cut rounds with
- Pastry brush
- Cooling rack

Method:
1. Preheat oven to gas mark 6 / 200C / 400F.
2. *If using sweet rich shortcrust pastry*: break off a piece that can be rolled into a ball the size of a walnut and press into one indent in patty tin so that it covers the base and sides. Repeat this for all 12 indents in each tin (use same tin twice if you only have one).
3. *If using shortcrust pastry*: roll out using a rolling pin to around ¼ inch thick and use a large pastry cutter to

create the bases, then a slightly smaller pastry cutter for the lids. You should have around 24 of each.

4. Put 1tsp on mincemeat in each pastry lining and flatten out slightly.

5. *If using sweet rich shortcrust pastry recipe*: break off slightly smaller pieces for the lids (divide remaining dough into the number of lids required first) and flatten into circles between palms of hands. Place on top of bases in patty tin and press down lightly – there is no need to use milk to seal.

6. *If using shortcrust pastry*: brush a small amount of milk / beaten egg around each lid and press lightly onto bases.

7. Brush tops with milk/beaten egg and bake in top of oven for 15-20 minutes, or until golden brown.

8. Remove from oven and leave to cool in tin for 5 minutes, then remove to a wire rack to cool completely.

Brandy Butter

Brandy butter is an excellent accompaniment for hot mince pies or Christmas pudding. It is quite rich and high in alcohol content.

Ingredients:
- 4oz (113g) unsalted butter
- ½-1lb (440-900g) icing sugar (confectioner's/powdered sugar)
- Brandy to taste, added 1tbsp (15ml) at a time – the better the brandy, the smoother the taste

Equipment:
- Either a mixing bowl and a wooden spoon OR a food mixer
- Airtight container

Method:
1. Put butter in a large bowl and beat with a wooden spoon until the butter becomes light in colour and has a soft, creamy texture.
2. Sieve a quarter of the icing sugar into the bowl and add 1tbsp (15ml) of brandy. This *should* avoid curdling, but it doesn't matter too much. Beat until the mixture is smooth.
3. Continue to add the icing sugar and brandy to the bowl, beating together each time until all the icing sugar has been used.
4. Taste and adjust using more brandy and icing sugar, maintaining a texture similar to whipped cream.
5. Put in an airtight container and refrigerate. Brandy butter will keep for at least two weeks.

About Debbie McGowan

Debbie McGowan is an author and publisher based in a semi-rural corner of Lancashire, England. She writes character-driven, realist fiction, celebrating life, love and relationships. A working class girl, she 'ran away' to London at seventeen, was homeless, unemployed and then homeless again, interspersed with animal rights activism (all legal, honest ;)) and volunteer work as a mental health advocate. At twenty-five, she went back to college to study social science—tough with two toddlers, but they had a 'stay at home' dad, so it worked itself out. These days, the toddlers are young women (much to their chagrin), and Debbie teaches undergraduate students, writes novels and runs an independent publishing company, occasionally grabbing an hour of sleep where she can.

Find Debbie McGowan online:

Website: debbiemcgowan.co.uk
Newsletter Signup: eepurl.com/b8emHL
Blog: deb248211.blogspot.com
Facebook: facebook.com/
DebbieMcGowanAuthor andfacebook.com/
beatentrackpublishing
Twitter: @writerdebmcg
YouTube: youtube.com/deb248211
Instagram: instagram/writerdebmcg
Google+: plus.google.com/+DebbieMcGowan
Tumblr: writerdebmcg.tumblr.com
LinkedIn: uk.linkedin.com/in/writerdebmcg
Goodreads: goodreads.com/DebbieMcGowan

By Debbie McGowan

Checking Him Out Series
Checking Him Out (Book One)
Checking Him Out For the Holidays (Novella)
Hiding Out (Novella – Noah and Matty – HBTC Crossover)
Taking Him On (Book Two – Noah and Matty)
Checking In (Book Three)
The Making of Us (Book Four – Jesse and Leigh)

Seeds of Tyrone Series
~ co-written with Raine O'Tierney
Leaving Flowers (Book One)
Where the Grass is Greener (Book Two)
Christmas Craic and Mistletoe (Book Three)

Hiding Behind The Couch Series
The ongoing story of 'The Circle'…
Nine friends from high school;
Nine friends for life.

The Story So Far…
in chronological order:
novellas and short novels are 'stand-alone' stories, but tie in with the
series. Think Middle Earth—well, more Middle England, but with a
social conscience!

Beginnings (Novella)
Ruminations (Novel)
Class-A (Short Story)
Hiding Behind The Couch (Season One)
No Time Like The Present (Season Two)
The Harder They Fall (Season Three)
Crying in the Rain (Novel)

First Christmas (Novella)
In The Stars Part I: Capricorn–Gemini (Season Four)
Breaking Waves (Novella)
In The Stars Part II: Cancer–Sagittarius (Season Five)
A Midnight Clear (Novella)
Red Hot Christmas (Novella)
Two By Two (Season Six)
Hiding Out (Novella – CHO Crossover)
Breakfast at Cordelia's Aquarium (Short Story)
Chain of Secrets (Novella)
Those Jeffries Boys (Novel)
The WAG and The Scoundrel (Gray Fisher #1)
Reunions (Season Seven)
To Be Sure (Novella)
Tabula Rasa (Gray Fisher #2)
What A Scorcher! (Short Story)
Goth of Christmas Past (Novel)

Stand-Alone Stories
Champagne (LGBT Historical Novel)
'Time to Go' in *Story Salon Big Book of Stories (Contemporary Short Story)*
And The Walls Came Tumbling Down (Sci-fi Novel)
No Dice (Sci-fi Novel)
Double Six (Sci-fi Novel)
Sugar and Sawdust (M/M Romance Short Story)
Cherry Pop Valentine (M/M Romance Short Story)
Coming Up ~ co-written with Al Stewart (LGBT Short Story)
Of the Bauble (LGBT Fantasy Romance Novella)
So Long, Little Black Diamonds (Short (True) Story)
The Pastor's Last Drop (Historical Novel (Ongoing) – Wattpad)
When Skies Have Fallen (LGBT Historical Romance Novel)
A Snowy Ball (When Skies Have Fallen #1.5)
The Great Village Bun Fight (Contemporary Novella)

www.hidingbehindthecouch.com
www.debbiemcgowan.co.uk

Beaten Track Publishing

For more titles from Beaten Track Publishing,
please visit our website:

http://www.beatentrackpublishing.com

Thanks for reading!

PRAISE FOR M. L. BUCHMAN

Tom Clancy fans open to a strong female lead will clamor for more.

— *DRONE*, PUBLISHERS WEEKLY

Superb!

— *DRONE*, BOOKLIST STARRED REVIEW

The best military thriller I've read in a very long time. Love the female characters.

— *DRONE*, SHELDON MCARTHUR, FOUNDER OF THE MYSTERY BOOKSTORE, LA

A fabulous soaring thriller.

— *TAKE OVER AT MIDNIGHT*, MIDWEST BOOK REVIEW

Meticulously researched, hard-hitting, and suspenseful.

— *PURE HEAT*, PUBLISHERS WEEKLY, STARRED REVIEW

Expert technical details abound, as do realistic military missions with superb imagery that will have readers feeling as if they are right there in the midst and on the edges of their seats.

— *Light Up the Night*, RT Reviews, 4 1/2 stars

Buchman has catapulted his way to the top tier of my favorite authors.

— Fresh Fiction

Nonstop action that will keep readers on the edge of their seats.

— *Take Over at Midnight*, Library Journal

M L. Buchman's ability to keep the reader right in the middle of the action is amazing.

— Long and Short Reviews

The only thing you'll ask yourself is, "When does the next one come out?"

— *Wait Until Midnight*, RT Reviews, 4 stars